The Day the Computers Broke Down

Story by Laura Normand

Illustrations by Lori Anderson

RSVP
RAINTREE
STECK-VAUGHN
PUBLISHERS
The Steck-Vaughn Company

Austin, Texas

To all of my teachers and friends throughout the years who have
always been there with an encouraging word,
and to my family — without their love and support, I could never
be where I am today. — L.N.

To my children: Gregory, Ethan, and Janessa. — L.A.

Library of Congress Cataloging-in-Publication Data

Normand, Laura, 1983 –
     The day the computers broke down / story by
Laura Normand ; illustrations by Lori Anderson.
          p.   cm. — (Publish-a-book)
     Summary: When all the computers go out on her
birthday, Kerri's entire computer-controlled town shuts
down, but her old-fashioned grandmother saves the
day.
     ISBN 0–8172–4426–3
     1. Children's writings, American.   [1. Computers —
Fiction.   2. Birthdays — Fiction.   3. Children's
writings.]   I. Anderson, Lori, ill.   II. Title.   III. Series.
PZ7.N787Day   1996
[E]—dc20   95-43978
                                              CIP   AC

Little Kerri Greyson cautiously opened one eye, then the other, and sighed. She hadn't fallen asleep. How could she? After all, tomorrow was her sixth birthday. Listening to the familiar hum of the city's power generators, she was too excited to sleep. Suddenly, the humming stopped, and her night light clicked off, leaving her in darkness.

5

Kerri crawled out of bed and made her way blindly
to her parents' bedroom. She shook her mother awake
and pointed out the window.

"Mommy, look."

Yawning, Mrs. Greyson did as her daughter
requested. She sat up straight, taking a closer look.

"All of the power's off," Kerri's mom said,
bewildered. "This couldn't have happened unless—"
Then she realized it. "The computers have broken down."

As daylight approached, Mr. Greyson was explaining to Kerri what happened.

"Computers control our town," he began. "If something goes wrong, everything goes off, like the security matrix, communications systems, television networks. . . . So I can't go to work, and you can't go to school."

Kerri grinned. Her dad always used big words. But, she was glad she used only computers in school, instead of textbooks like in the old days when Grandma went. Without the computers working, school was closed!

Kerri nodded, blissfully aware of the fact that her whole family could stay home for her birthday. Suddenly, another thought jumped into her mind.

"When is everyone else coming?"

Her mother and father exchanged nervous glances.

"They . . . they probably won't be able to make it," her mother said apologetically.

"Why?" Kerri demanded.

Her mother sighed. "The monorails are controlled by computer," she said. "With the computers out, the monorails that were supposed to bring everyone here for your birthday . . . well, they aren't running."

Kerri's blue eyes filled with tears, but she raced upstairs to her room before anyone could see them. Without thinking, she turned on her computer. The screen didn't light up. Then she remembered. She couldn't do <u>anything</u> without computers!

Downstairs, Kerri's parents were desperately trying to find a way to make their daughter's birthday better.

"We should call someplace and rent a car," Mr. Greyson suggested, "so we could pick up our relatives and bring them over here!"

"We can't," Mrs. Greyson replied tiredly. "The phone's hooked up to a main computer. I can't even order Kerri a cake." She gestured to the computer that she programmed her shopping lists into. When the grocery store computer received her order, it had someone deliver the items.

The two discouraged parents slumped in their seats, feeling useless.

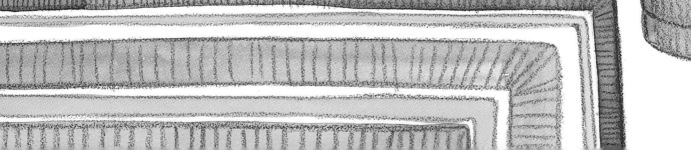

The day dragged on, and Kerri frequently checked her computer in the hopes that it would be working. It wasn't. Depressed, she finally sat down on the stairs.

A horn blared. Kerri's dad got up and opened the door to see what was happening. He was nearly trampled by a crowd of people piling into the house, singing a rousing chorus of "Happy Birthday to You." Kerri, who had been watching from the stairs, bounded down the steps. Her face lit up when she saw the presents and a plate of cookies.

"I thought you said no one could come!" she said to her mother happily.

Mrs. Greyson, just as astonished, greeted the relatives who had burst into her house so unexpectedly. Then she saw Grandma Esther, and her face broke into a knowing grin.

"Mom, how'd you do this?" Mrs. Greyson asked.

"Not that big a deal," Grandma Esther said in her typical no-nonsense way. "I'm practically the only one these days who still uses a gasoline-powered car, so I figured I'd put it to some use. What better way than to bring all our relatives to my granddaughter's birthday?"

"You're a lifesaver, Mom," Mrs. Greyson said, hugging Grandma Esther.

"I always said we shouldn't depend on those computers," Grandma grumbled. "I almost didn't make it here because those mechanics didn't know what to do without their machinery. My car was coughing and sputtering the whole way here," she sniffed disapprovingly. "Like I always say, old ways are better."

Before she could continue, Kerri raced up, shouting "Grandma!" with Mr. Greyson in hot pursuit. Both were smiling.

"When can we eat the cookies?" Kerri asked excitedly.

"Soon," Grandma said, chuckling. "I made them myself, you know. I went to the store yesterday to get the ingredients." She looked at her daughter, then smiled good-naturedly. "But first, Kerri, what do you say we open some presents?"

Kerri smiled.

Kerri received mainly computer games, which were many kids' favorite entertainment. Kerri was delighted at first, but then sadly realized that she couldn't use them today.

Last, she came to Grandma Esther's present. She unwrapped it, and gasped. A doll? She hadn't wanted a doll. What fun was a doll next to a computer game? Then she realized. She couldn't play with her computer today, but a doll . . .

Kerri's mouth slowly spread into a grin. Her grandmother smiled back.

"Thanks, Mom," Mrs. Greyson thought to herself. "You really saved the day with a little old-fashioned common sense."

Two hours later, the relatives had left. Mrs. Greyson was reading a novel, which she hadn't done in years, Mr. Greyson was contentedly working an old crossword puzzle, which he hadn't done in ages, and Kerri was happily playing with her doll. In fact, they didn't even notice when the computers came back on.

Twelve-year-old Laura Normand, author of **The Day the Computers Broke Down**, has had a great year. After being cast as the lead of the show *Annie* with a community theater, she won the town spelling bee. But she thinks winning the 1995 Publish-a-Book™ Contest is more than she could have hoped for. After all, Laura has dreamt of becoming an author since she was in first grade. This story idea came easily, since Laura has always thought of computers as an important part of the future.

Laura's homeroom teacher at Henry Barnard Elementary School, Karen Forsyth, encouraged her to enter the Publish-a-Book™ Contest. After Laura wrote the story, Elizabeth Trapanese, who works as one of the school's special reading teachers, sponsored her in the contest and helped her through the revision and editing process. Laura likes to credit them, and all of the other teachers who have encouraged her, with her success.

Laura was also chosen as the recipient of the 1995 Alexander Fischbein Young Writer's Award. This award was established in memory of Alex Fischbein, a writer who died at the age of ten, to encourage young students to write and submit their works for publication.

When she is not writing, Laura enjoys reading, playing the piano, horseback riding, acting and singing in community theater, and much more. She lives in Enfield, Connecticut, with her parents, Linda and Steven Normand, her 15-year-old brother, Brad, and their two dogs, Sandy and Kempa.

In the future, Laura wants to continue writing, and she hopes to be published again. Besides being an author, she plans to do other things when she's older. What those other things may be? The possibilities for her future are endless.

The twenty honorable-mention winners in the **1995 Raintree/Steck-Vaughn Publish-a-Book™ Contest** were Mike Asmar, Boulan Park Middle School, Troy, Michigan; Catie Myers-Wood, Grey Culbreth Middle School, Chapel Hill, North Carolina; Stephanie Iannucci, St. Callistus School, Philadelphia, Pennsylvania; Mavis Morse, Hermon Elementary School, Bangor, Maine; Tina Addington, Rorimer Elementary School, LaPuente, California; Fred Barr, Cape Christian Academy, Cape May, New Jersey; Benjamin J. Brotsker, E. A. Tighe School, Margate, New Jersey; Katherine E. Coons, Haycock Elementary School, Falls Church, Virginia; Marwin Hunte, P.S. 203, Brooklyn, New York; Gary Kenneth Burrell, Jr., Sinclair Lane Elementary School, Baltimore, Maryland; Mary Elizabeth Smith, St. Rose of Lima School, Haddon Heights, New Jersey; Jonathan P. Walsh, Haycock Elementary School, Falls Church, Virginia; Daniel Ross Walt, Quincy Public Library, Quincy, Illinois; Brynn Cahill, Central Middle School, San Carlos, California; Emmy Ogle, Sierra Oaks School, Sacramento, California; Nicholas A. Langston, Iuka Elementary School, Iuka, Mississippi; Kate Zimmermann, M. H. Burnett Elementary School, Wilmington, Delaware; Allison Condon, Peter Noyes School, Sudbury, Massachusetts; Ryan Dixon, Riverside Elementary School, Moorhead, Minnesota; Julie Young, St. Ann's Academy, Calhoun, Georgia.

Lori Anderson was born on the West Coast, but has spent most of her life in the southwestern United States. An illustrator for fifteen years, she lives in Provo, Utah, and teaches design and illustration at Brigham Young University. She has six wonderful children, three older and three under the age of five. Lori has been active in numerous community art projects for children. She loves art in its various forms — film, drama, literature, dance, sculpture, and jewelry making — and likes to travel, seeking adventure wherever she goes.